10/13

Presidents of the United States Bio-Graphics

John Adams
2nd U.S. President

Written by **Joeming Dunn** Illustrated by **Rod Espinosa**

magic Wagon

visit us at www.abdopublishing.com

Published by Magic Wagon, a division of the ABDO Publishing Group, 8000 West 78th Street, Edina, Minnesota 55439. Copyright © 2012 by Abdo Consulting Group, Inc. International copyrights reserved in all countries. All rights reserved. No part of this book may be reproduced in any form without written permission from the publisher.

Graphic Planet™ is a trademark and logo of Magic Wagon.

Printed in the United States of America, North Mankato, Minnesota.
042011
092011
♻ This book contains at least 10% recycled materials.

Written by Joeming Dunn
Illustrated and colored by Rod Espinosa
Lettered by Rod Espinosa
Edited by Stephanie Hedlund and Rochelle Baltzer
Interior layout and design by Antarctic Press
Cover art by Ben Dunn
Cover design by Abbey Fitzgerald

Library of Congress Cataloging-in-Publication Data

Dunn, Joeming W.
  John Adams : 2nd U.S. president / written by Joeming Dunn ; illustrated by Rod Espinosa.
      p. cm. -- (Presidents of the United States bio-graphics)
  Includes index.
  ISBN 978-1-61641-644-7
  1. Adams, John, 1735-1826--Juvenile literature. 2. Presidents--United States--Biography--Juvenile literature. 3. Adams, John, 1735-1826--Comic books, strips, etc. 4. Presidents--United States--Biography--Comic books, strips, etc. 5. Graphic novels. I. Espinosa, Rod, ill. II. Title.
  E322.D86 2012
  973.4'4092--dc22
  [B]

                                   2011010673

Table of Contents

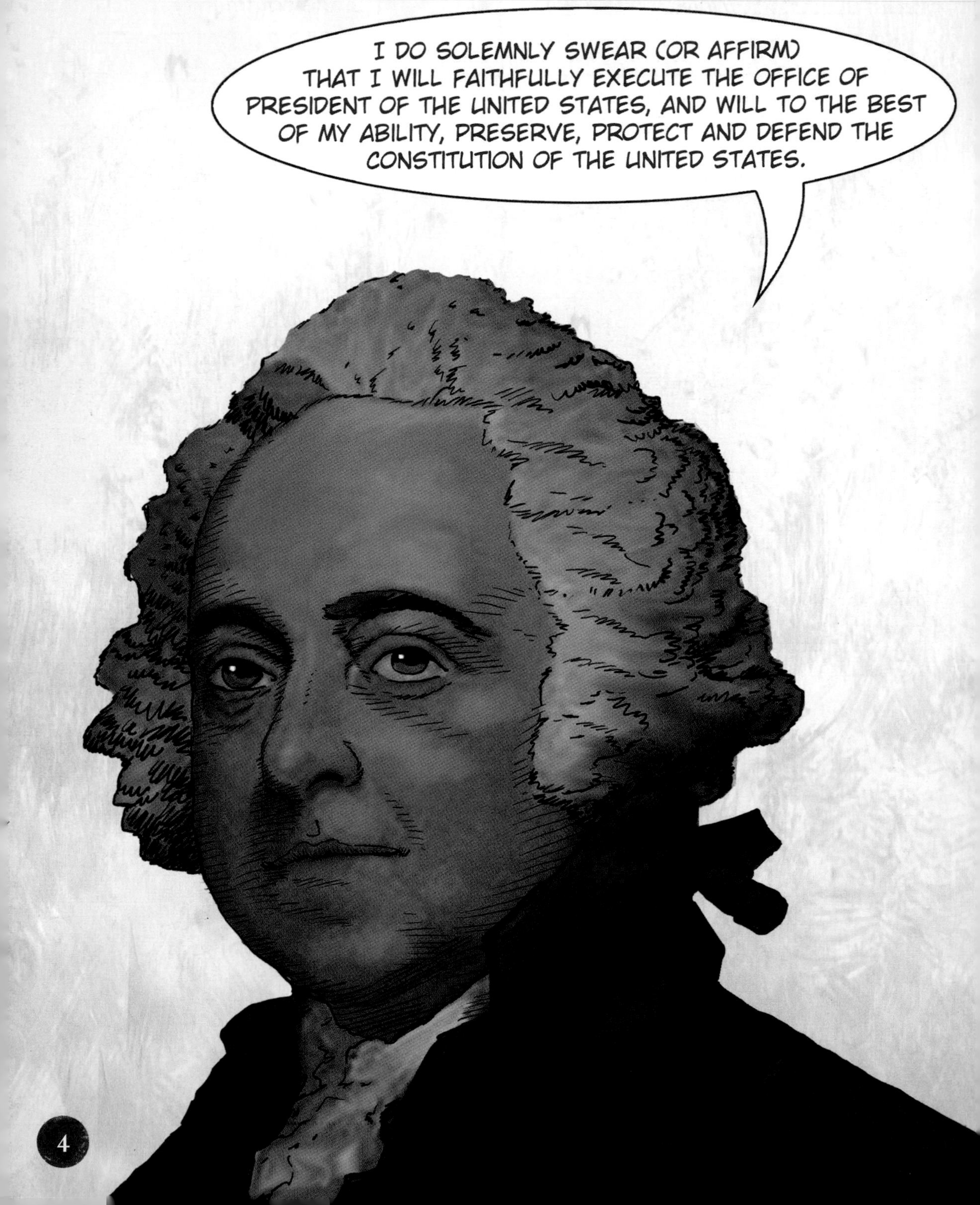
I DO SOLEMNLY SWEAR (OR AFFIRM) THAT I WILL FAITHFULLY EXECUTE THE OFFICE OF PRESIDENT OF THE UNITED STATES, AND WILL TO THE BEST OF MY ABILITY, PRESERVE, PROTECT AND DEFEND THE CONSTITUTION OF THE UNITED STATES.

John Adams was born in Braintree, Massachusetts, on October 30, 1735. His parents were John Adams and Susanna Boylston.

His father was a farmer, a deacon, and a leader of the community.

The Adams family came from Puritan settlers. Young Adams was encouraged to become a minister.

John Adams had a quiet childhood. At the age of 16, he entered Harvard College. He graduated from Harvard in 1755.

I BELIEVE IT WOULD BE THE BEST USE OF YOUR TALENTS.

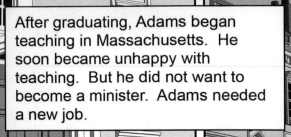

After graduating, Adams began teaching in Massachusetts. He soon became unhappy with teaching. But he did not want to become a minister. Adams needed a new job.

In 1758, Adams was admitted to the bar. He started his own law practice in Braintree, Massachusetts. He often traveled from Braintree to Boston for work.

Adams next became an apprentice to James Putnam, a well-known lawyer.

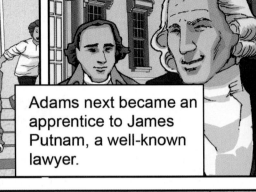

Soon, John Adams met Abigail Smith. The young couple fell in love. They were married on October 25, 1764.

John and Abigail Adams had six children. But only four of them survived to become adults.

Abigail was very independent and smart. Her husband came to her with all of his troubles. Many letters between the two show their love during this difficult period in America.

From 1754 to 1763, the British and French fought in the French and Indian War. They fought over land in North America.

After the war, the British government had a lot of debt. The British decided to tax the American colonies to pay for the war.

NEW TAXES

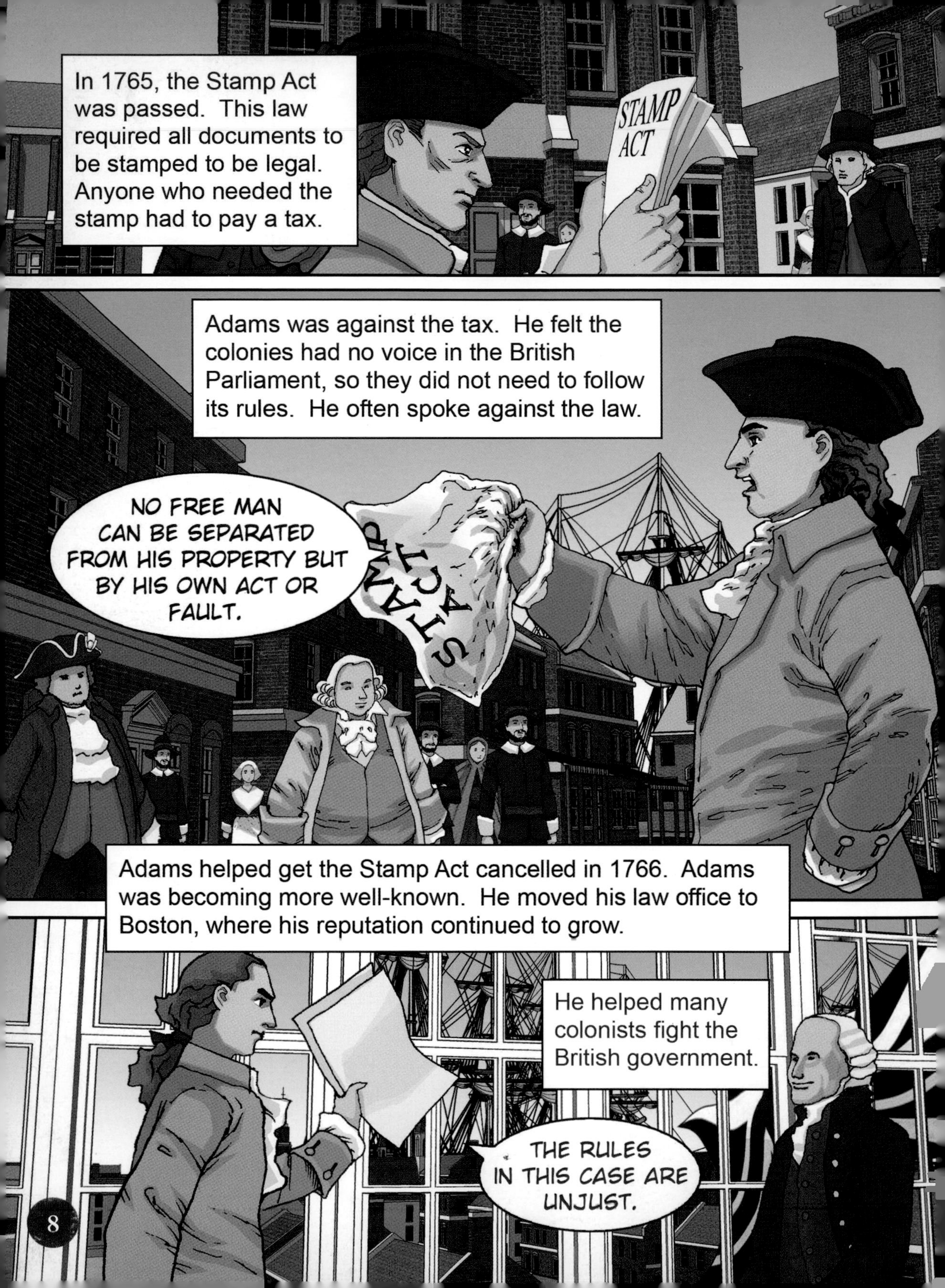
In 1765, the Stamp Act was passed. This law required all documents to be stamped to be legal. Anyone who needed the stamp had to pay a tax.
STAMP ACT
Adams was against the tax. He felt the colonies had no voice in the British Parliament, so they did not need to follow its rules. He often spoke against the law.
NO FREE MAN CAN BE SEPARATED FROM HIS PROPERTY BUT BY HIS OWN ACT OR FAULT.
STAMP ACT
Adams helped get the Stamp Act cancelled in 1766. Adams was becoming more well-known. He moved his law office to Boston, where his reputation continued to grow.
He helped many colonists fight the British government.
THE RULES IN THIS CASE ARE UNJUST.

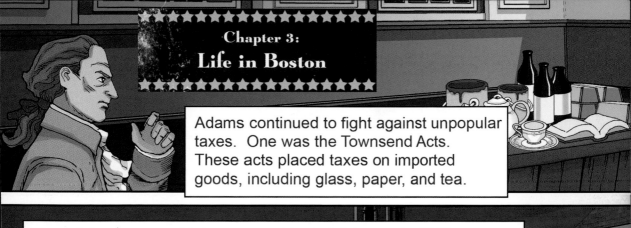

Adams continued to fight against unpopular taxes. One was the Townsend Acts. These acts placed taxes on imported goods, including glass, paper, and tea.

Though he was a patriot, one event tested Adams. In 1770, a group of British soldiers fired upon a mob of angry Bostonians, killing five of them. This event became known as the Boston Massacre.

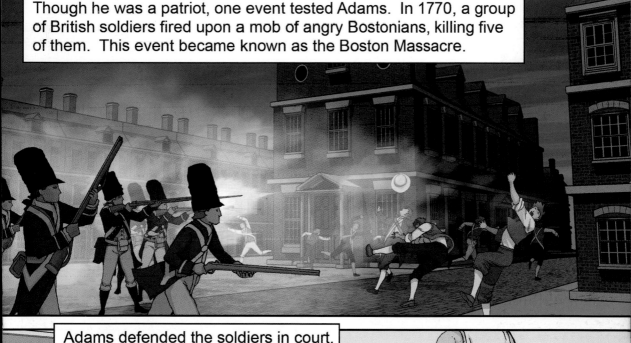

Adams defended the soldiers in court. He said the soldiers were provoked.

MY CLIENTS ARE INNOCENT.

Only two of the soldiers were found guilty. The other soldiers were set free. Some people did not agree with Adams's actions. But many praised his dedication to justice.

Adams didn't let this upset him. He again fought against British rules.

He supported acts of rebellion like the Boston Tea Party in 1773. During the Boston Tea Party, colonists threw tea into Boston Harbor in response to a tax on the tea.

In 1774, Adams got an important opportunity. He and his cousin Samuel Adams were elected as delegates to the First Continental Congress. It had representatives from 12 of the 13 colonies.

The First Continental Congress met to discuss the acts set by the British government.

These acts included the Intolerable Acts and the Boston Port Act. This act closed Boston Harbor in response to the Boston Tea Party.

The Congress also discussed the Massachusetts Government Act. It put the colony under the control of the British government.

Finally, they talked about the Quartering Act. It forced colonists to house British soldiers.

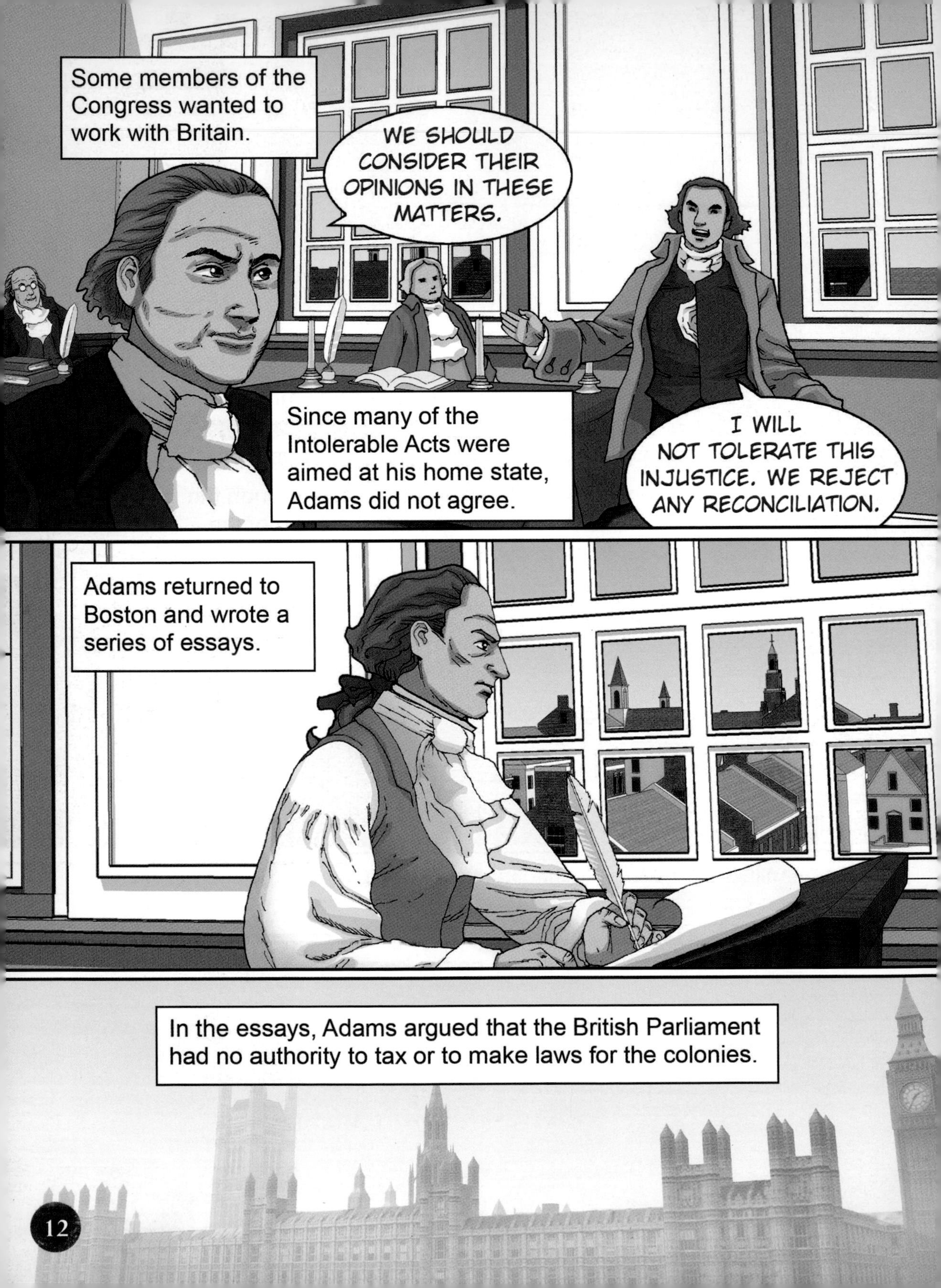

Some members of the Congress wanted to work with Britain.
WE SHOULD CONSIDER THEIR OPINIONS IN THESE MATTERS.
Since many of the Intolerable Acts were aimed at his home state, Adams did not agree.
I WILL NOT TOLERATE THIS INJUSTICE. WE REJECT ANY RECONCILIATION.
Adams returned to Boston and wrote a series of essays.
In the essays, Adams argued that the British Parliament had no authority to tax or to make laws for the colonies.

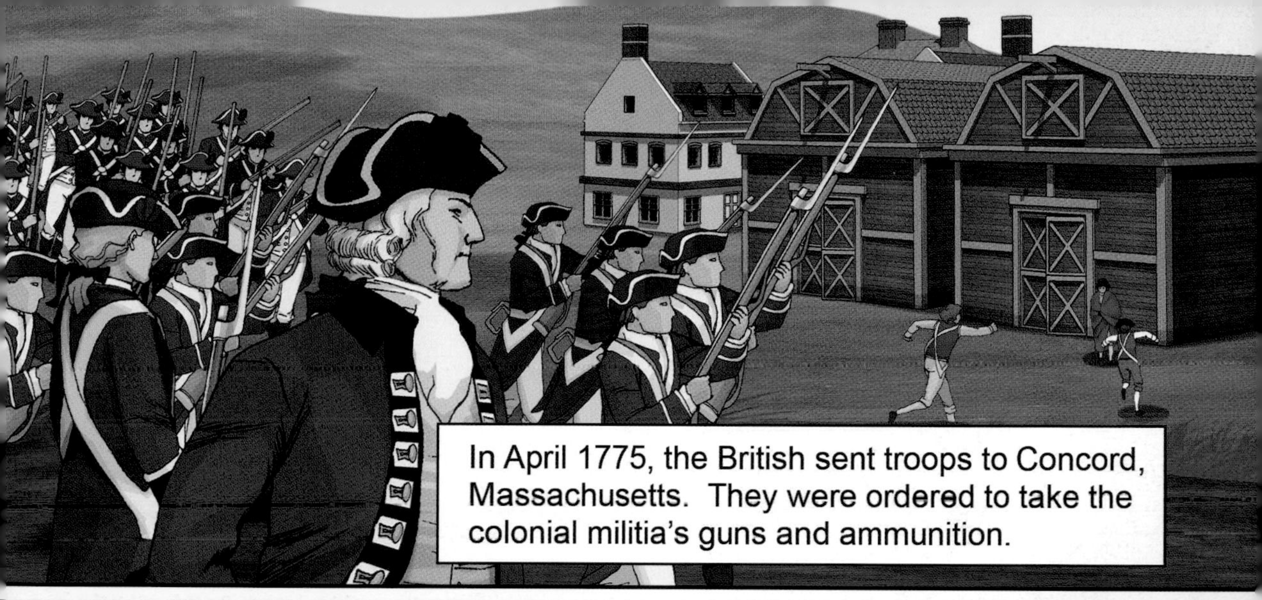
In April 1775, the British sent troops to Concord, Massachusetts. They were ordered to take the colonial militia's guns and ammunition.

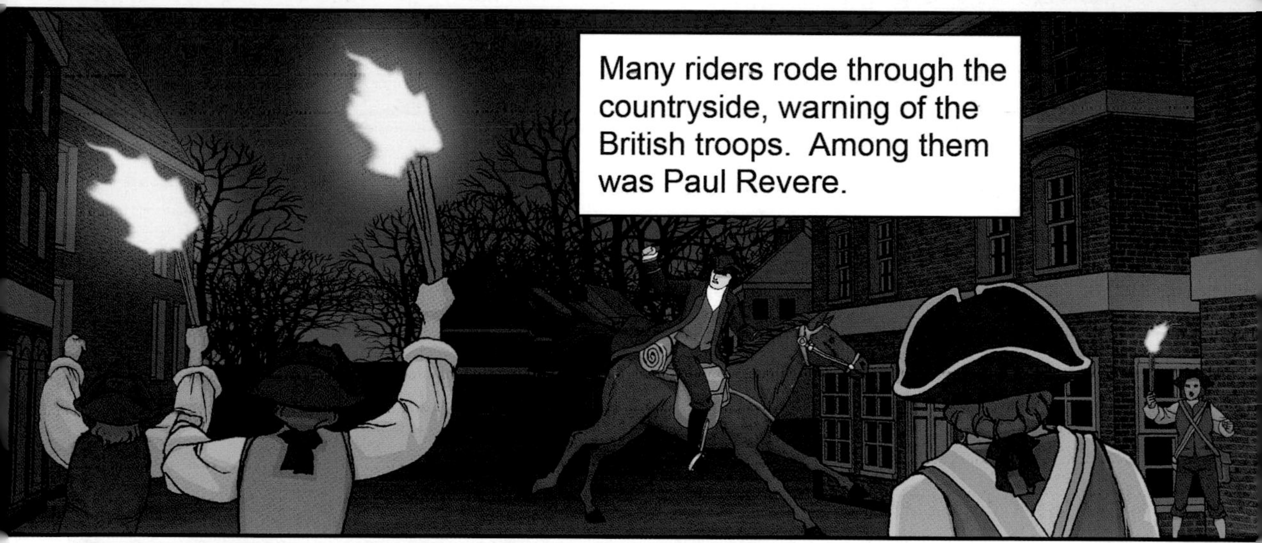
Many riders rode through the countryside, warning of the British troops. Among them was Paul Revere.

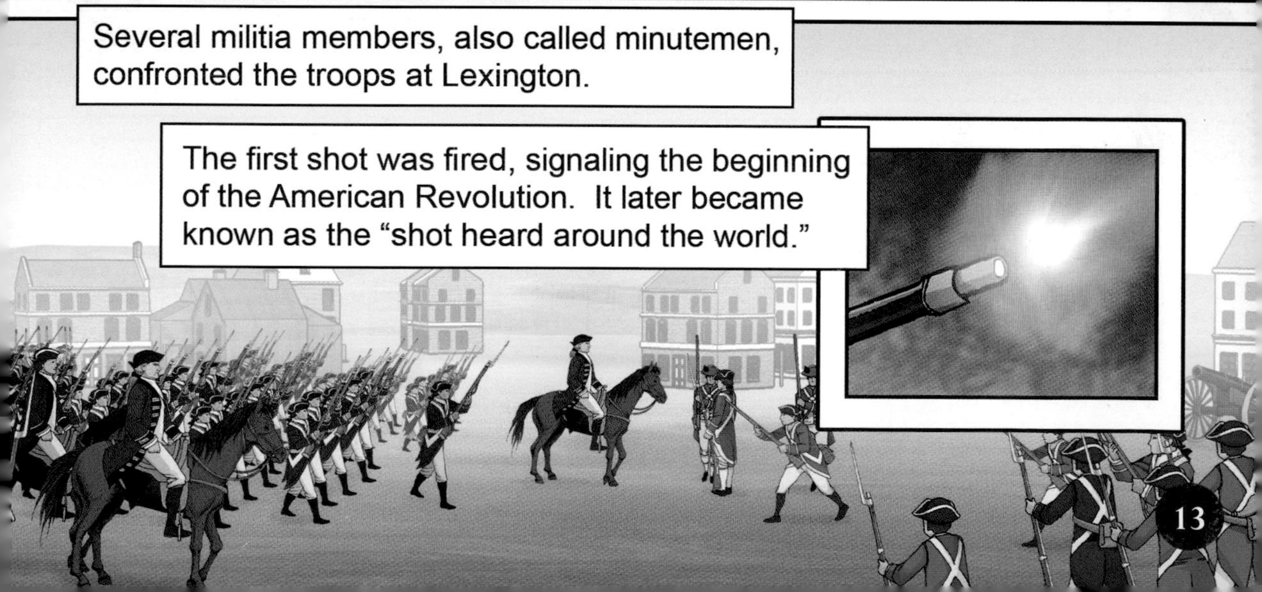
Several militia members, also called minutemen, confronted the troops at Lexington.
The first shot was fired, signaling the beginning of the American Revolution. It later became known as the "shot heard around the world."

Chapter 5: The Second Continental Congress

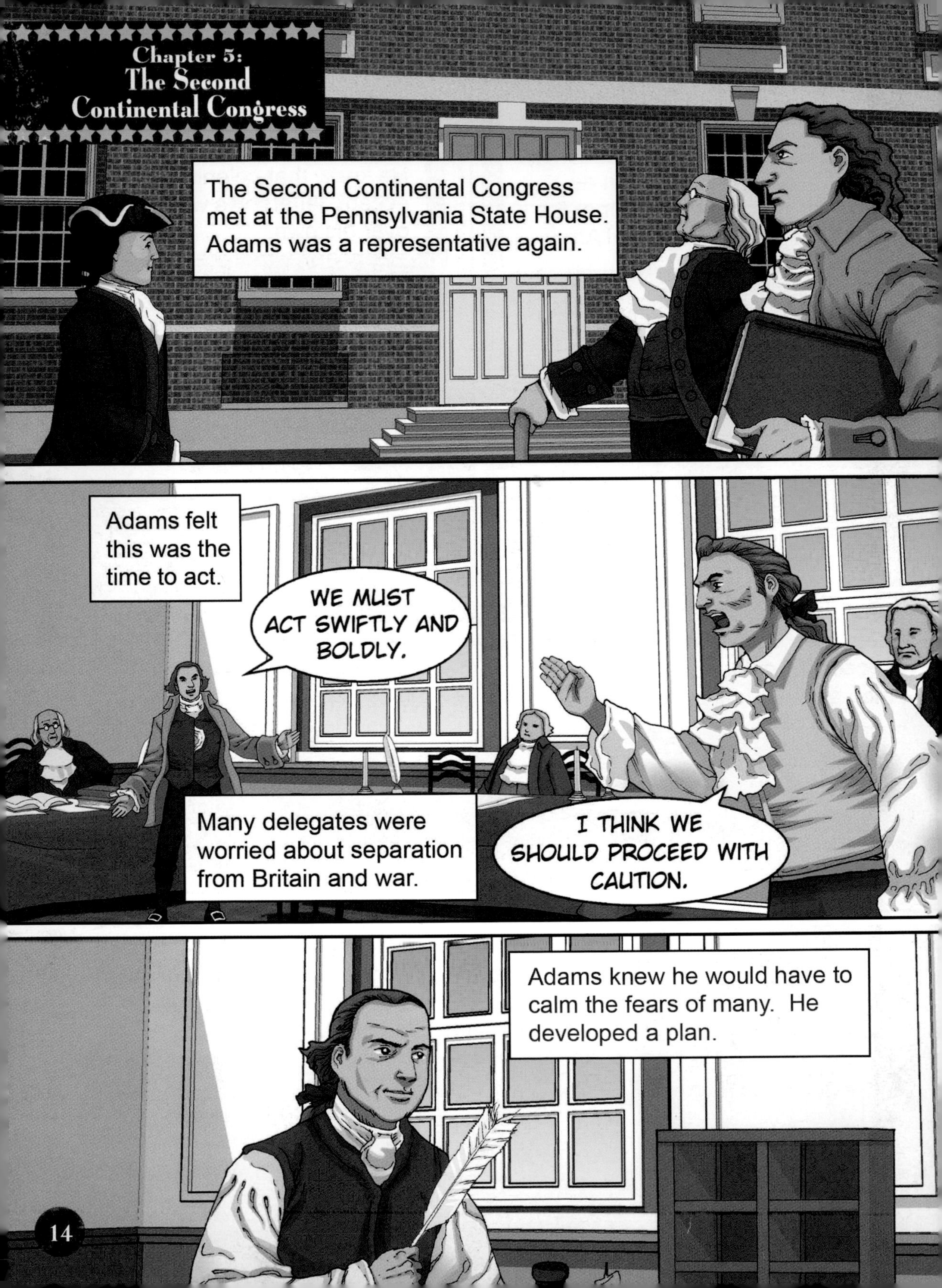
The Second Continental Congress met at the Pennsylvania State House. Adams was a representative again.
Adams felt this was the time to act.
WE MUST ACT SWIFTLY AND BOLDLY.
Many delegates were worried about separation from Britain and war.
I THINK WE SHOULD PROCEED WITH CAUTION.
Adams knew he would have to calm the fears of many. He developed a plan.

The first thing Adams did was recommend George Washington as commander of the Continental Army.

Next, Adams suggested that Thomas Jefferson write the Declaration of Independence. He knew that colonists would accept Jefferson's writing over his own.

Both men were from Virginia, one of the earliest and most successful colonies. Adams knew that this would give the men a great deal of influence over the other delegates.

In early July 1776, Adams read Jefferson's draft of the Declaration of Independence. He debated several parts of it. Once the Second Continental Congress had discussed these points, Adams demanded action for the document.

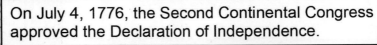

On July 4, 1776, the Second Continental Congress approved the Declaration of Independence.

Adams wrote to Abigail about the event. He said there should be "pomp and parade... bonfires and illuminations from one end of this continent to the other from this time forward."

Early on, Adams was chosen to head the Board of War and Ordnance. This board helped supply the army and create the navy.

He then went to France to ask for help in the war.

When he arrived, Adams found that Benjamin Franklin had already made a treaty with France.

Adams returned to Massachusetts. There, he helped create the state's constitution. It became the model for other state constitutions.

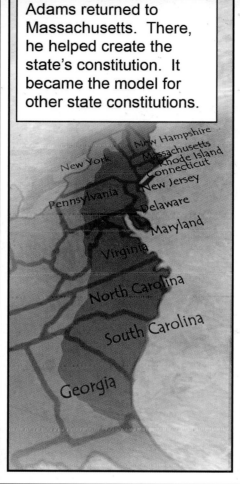

New Hampshire
New York
Massachusetts
Rhode Island
Connecticut
New Jersey
Pennsylvania
Delaware
Maryland
Virginia
North Carolina
South Carolina
Georgia

Adams believed no part of the government should have too much control. This is called separation of powers.

That idea shaped the U.S. Constitution.

In October 1781, General George Washington and his army surrounded British general Charles Cornwallis at Yorktown. Cornwallis eventually surrendered.

Adams and Franklin were sent to Paris, France. There, they began discussing a peace treaty with Great Britain.

Adams's fiery style and Franklin's calmness worked well together. They soon had signed the Treaty of Paris. It officially ended the American Revolution in 1783.

The Treaty of Paris forced Britain to recognize America as a sovereign nation. It also extended the border of the United States to the Mississippi River.

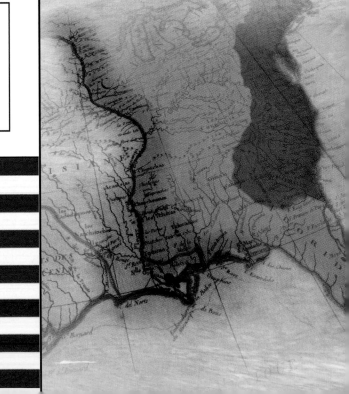

Adams remained in Europe to become the first minister to Great Britain. While there, he studied and traveled. He also wrote a book.

Thomas Jefferson joined Adams in Paris in 1784. The two men soon became very close friends. They joined forces to negotiate with many of the European countries.

Adams returned to the United States in 1788. By then, the Constitution had been written and had begun its journey to ratification.

When the Constitution was finally ratified, the first order of business was to elect the first president and vice president. This was done under a new system called the Electoral College.

In the first election in 1789, each state sent delegates who had two votes. The person with the most votes became president, and the person with the second-highest amount became vice president. George Washington received votes from all the delegates and became the first president of the United States.

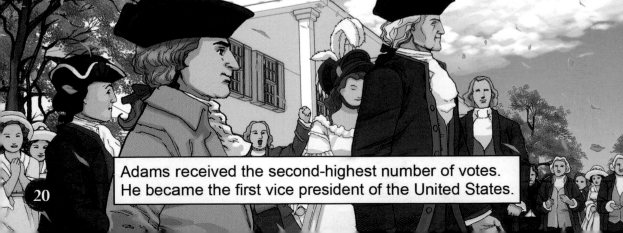

Adams received the second-highest number of votes. He became the first vice president of the United States.

Adams disliked being vice president. Most of his duties involved breaking tie votes in the Senate.

THIS IS THE MOST INSIGNIFICANT OFFICE THAT EVER THE INVENTION OF MAN CONTRIVED OR HIS IMAGINATION CONCEIVED.

Adams became a member of the Federalist Party, which was led by Alexander Hamilton. The Federalists believed in a strong central government.

Federalists also wanted a central banking system for economic stability.

BANK

And they supported the Jay Treaty. This treaty tried to solve many of the issues between the United States and Great Britain after the revolution.

Opposite the Federalists were the Democratic-Republicans. Their leaders were Thomas Jefferson and James Madison. They favored states' rights and thought the Jay Treaty was too friendly to Britain.

Adams agreed with more of the Federalist ideas, but he tried to work with both groups.

WE MUST ALL WORK TOGETHER.

In 1796, Washington decided not to run for a third term. He supported Adams as the next president.

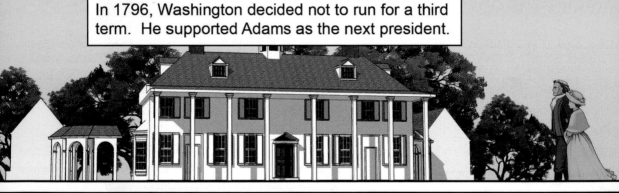

Thomas Jefferson also wanted to run for president. For the first time, there would be a race for the office.

In a very close election, Adams defeated Jefferson. Adams became the second president of the United States.

Jefferson became the vice president. Adams tried to work with Jefferson, but Jefferson chose to remain independent.

Almost immediately into Adams's term, the United States was on the brink of war. France began boarding and robbing American ships.

Adams sent three men to negotiate with France's foreign minister, Charles de Talleyrand.

Three French agents, known as X, Y, and Z, would not talk unless they received a bribe.

Many Americans called for war against France.

Adams instead suspended trade with France. He ordered an increase of troops and began building a navy.

Many people disagreed with Adams. Next, he passed the Alien and Sedition Acts. These acts allowed the government to jail newspaper editors who wrote against the government. Many thought it was a way to silence anyone against Adams.

Adams knew the new nation was not strong enough for war. So, he sent another group to France, led by William Vans Murray. This group successfully negotiated a treaty with France.

In the election of 1800, John Adams and Charles Pinckney ran for the Federalists. They ran against the Democratic-Republicans Thomas Jefferson and Aaron Burr.

The campaign was tough for Adams. Many believed he was weakened by not declaring war and by trying to suppress free speech with the Alien and Sedition Acts.

When the Electoral College met, Jefferson and Adams each had the same number of votes. So, the contest was decided in the House of Representatives. Jefferson was eventually elected president.

In one of Adams's last acts as president, he appointed several Federalists as judges. This became known as the Midnight Appointments.

After leaving office, Adams returned to his hometown. He began reading about and writing on a variety of topics.

Over time, Adams exchanged letters with Jefferson, renewing their friendship.

Adams had the pleasure of seeing his son John Quincy Adams be elected president in 1824.

July 4, 1826, was the fiftieth anniversary of the Declaration of Independence. That day, John Adams lay resting in his home in Quincy, Massachusetts. When told about the date, he stated it was a good day and soon after passed away.

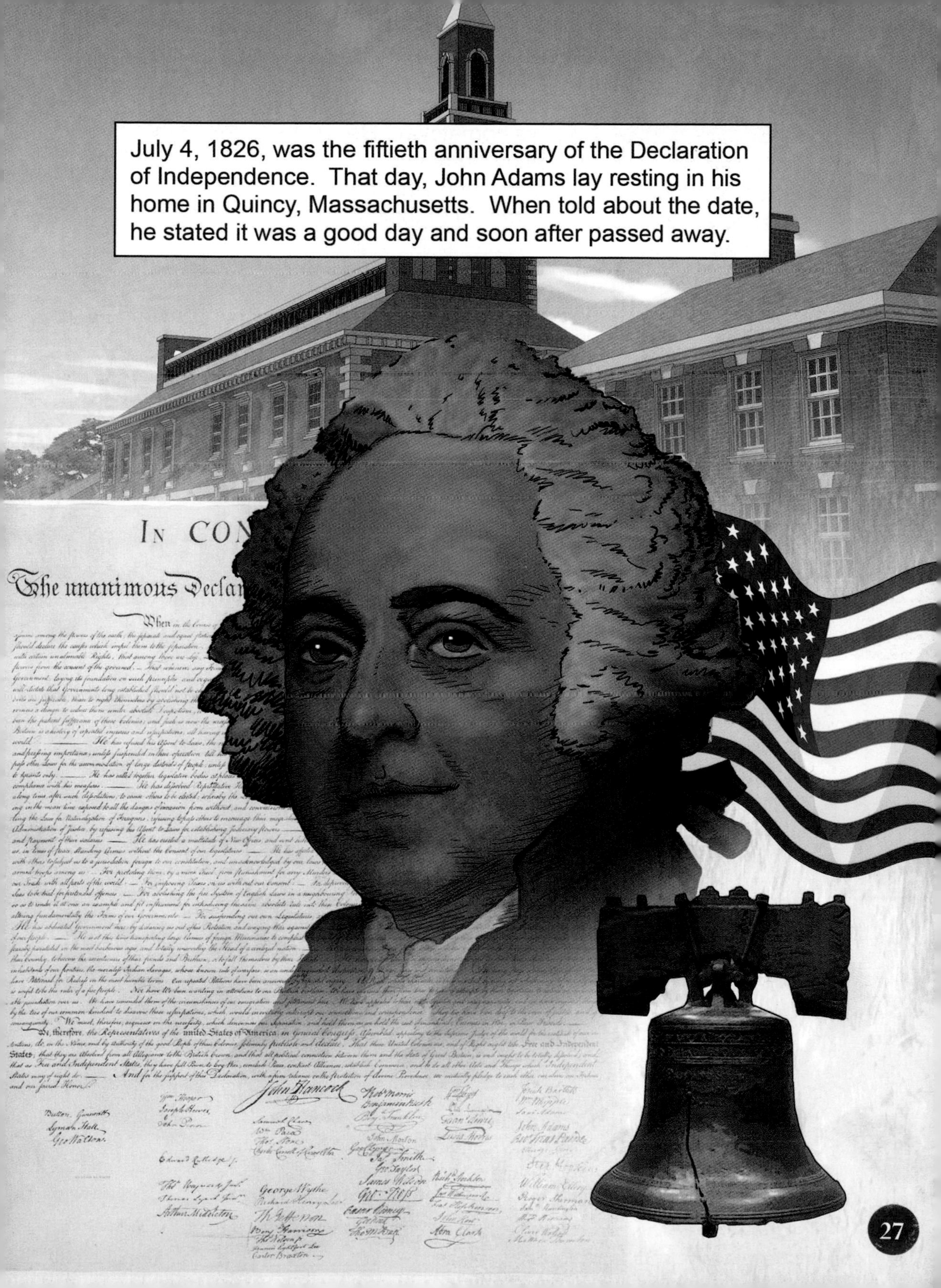
IN CON
The unanimous Declar

Name - John Adams   Born - October 30, 1735

Wife - Abigail Smith (1744–1818)   Children - 6

Political Party - Federalist

Age at Inauguration - 61   Years Served - 1797–1801

Vice President - Thomas Jefferson

Died - July 4, 1826, age 90

President Adams's Cabinet

March 4, 1797 - March 3, 1801

State – Timothy Pickering; John Marshall (from June 6, 1800)

Treasury – Oliver Wolcott, Jr.; Samuel Dexter (from January 1, 1801)

War – James McHenry; Samuel Dexter (from May 13, 1800)

Attorney General – Charles Lee

Navy – Benjamin Stoddert

• To be president, a person must meet three requirements. He or she must be at least 35 years old and a natural-born U.S. citizen. A candidate must also have lived in the United States for at least 14 years.

• The U.S. presidential election is an indirect election. Voters from each state elect representatives called electors for the Electoral College. The number of electors is based on population. Each elector pledges to cast their vote for the candidate who receives the highest number of popular votes in their state. A candidate must receive the majority of Electoral College votes to win.

• Each president may be elected to two four-year terms. The presidential election is held on the Tuesday after the first Monday in November. The president is sworn in on January 20 of the following year.

• While in office, the president receives a salary of $400,000 each year. He or she lives in the White House and has 24-hour Secret Service protection. When the president leaves office, he or she receives Secret Service protection for ten more years. He or she also receives a yearly pension of $191,300 and funding for office space, supplies, and staff.

Timeline

1735 - John Adams was born on October 30 in Braintree, Massachusetts.

1755 - Adams graduated from Harvard College.

1758 - Adams started his own law practice in Braintree.

1764 - Adams married Abigail Smith on October 25.

1765 - Parliament set the Stamp Act on the colonies.

1766 - The Stamp Act was repealed; Adams moved his law office to Boston.

1770 - Adams defended the Boston Massacre soldiers in court.

1773 - The Boston Tea Party occurred in December.

1774 - Adams was elected to the First Continental Congress.

1775 - Adams was elected to the Second Continental Congress. He nominated George Washington to lead the Continental Army and Thomas Jefferson to write the Declaration of Independence.

1776 - The Declaration of Independence was approved on July 4.

1783 - Adams and Benjamin Franklin signed the Treaty of Paris, recognizing America as a nation.

1789 - Adams was elected the first vice president.

1796 - Adams was elected the 2nd U.S. President.

1800 - Adams lost a very close election against Jefferson for president.

1826 - Adams died on July 4 in his home.

Web Sites

To learn more about John Adams, visit ABDO Publishing Group online at **www.abdopublishing.com**. Web sites about Adams are featured on our Book Links page. These links are routinely monitored and updated to provide the most current information available.

Glossary

apprentice - a person who learns a trade or a craft from a skilled worker.

Constitution - the laws that govern the United States.

Continental Congress - the body of representatives who spoke for and acted on behalf of the 13 colonies.

debate - to argue publicly about a question or a topic.

debt - something owed to someone, especially money.

delegate - a person chosen to represent others.

Democratic-Republican - a member of the Democratic-Republican party of the early 1800s. Democratic-Republicans believed in weak national government and strong state government.

Electoral College - the group of representatives that elects the U.S. president and vice president by casting electoral votes. Each state has a certain number of representatives, or electors, based on population. Electors cast their votes for the candidate who received the most popular votes in their state.

Federalist - a member of the Federalist political party. During the early 1800s, Federalists favored a strong national government.

import - to bring in goods from another country for sale or use.

insignificant - lacking position or influence.

militia (muh-LIH-shuh) - an army of citizens trained for emergencies and national defense.

negotiate (nih-GOH-shee-ayt) - to work out an agreement about the terms of something.

practice - a professional business.

provoke - to stir up purposely.

Puritan - a member of a religious group of the 1500s and 1600s. Puritans wanted simpler ceremonies and higher moral standards than those of the Church of England.

ratify - to officially approve.

reconciliation - to make up or become friends again.

sovereign - being independent.

suppress - to stop something from being said or done.

Index